GEORGE AND THE
DRAGON

CHRIS WORMELL

Alfred A. Knopf • New York

Far, far away in the high, high mountains

in a deep, deep valley in a dark, dark cave...

there lived a mighty dragon.

He could fly higher than the clouds

and faster than all the birds.

He could burn down a forest

with a blast of his fiery breath.

He could smash a castle wall

with a flick of his mighty tail.

And he could brush away an army

with a sweep of his monstrous wing.

There was nothing so fierce and so terrible
as the mighty dragon.

But he had a secret. A big secret—well,
actually, a very small secret...

he was terrified of mice!

Which was a pity, because that very day a
mouse moved into the cave just next door.

His name was George.

Now, George didn't much care for the cave next door. It was cold and dark and drafty.

The previous owner had been a bat,
so the fixtures and furnishings were
most inconvenient.

And the nearest cheese shop was
miles and miles away.

George was feeling rather miserable.
And to make matters worse...

he had NO SUGAR for his tea!

"I know," said George, "I'll just pop next
door and see if I can borrow some."
So he did.

"I say, you couldn't loan me a couple of lumps of sugar, could you?" asked George.

"AAAAAAAAAGH!" screamed the dragon.

And fled.

"Oh, no," groaned George. "No tea, then."

But George did get his tea after all, with
two lumps of sugar. And he got cheese, too.
And nuts and berries and biscuits

and crackers and cream cheese sandwiches
and jelly and ice cream and fairy cakes
with pink icing and...

a cozy little hole in the castle wall.

To John and Terry

THIS IS A BORZOI BOOK PUBLISHED BY ALFRED A. KNOPF
Copyright © 2002 by Chris Wormell
All rights reserved under International and Pan-American Copyright Conventions. Published in the
United States by Alfred A. Knopf, an imprint of Random House Children's Books, a division of Random
House, Inc., New York, and simultaneously in Canada by Random House of Canada Limited, Toronto.
Distributed by Random House, Inc., New York. Originally published in Great Britain in 2002 by Jonathan
Cape, an imprint of Random House Children's Books, a division of Random House, Inc.

KNOPF, BORZOI BOOKS, and the colophon are registered trademarks of Random House, Inc.

www.randomhouse.com/kids

Library of Congress Cataloging-in-Publication Data
Wormell, Christopher.
George and the dragon / Chris Wormell.
p.   cm.
SUMMARY: George the mouse unintentionally rids the kingdom of a ferocious dragon.
ISBN 0-375-83315-3 (trade) — ISBN 0-375-93315-8 (lib. bdg.)
[1. Mice—Fiction. 2. Dragons—Fiction.] I. Title.
PZ7.W88773Ge 2006
[E]—dc22
2004026360

MANUFACTURED IN CHINA
February 2006   First American Edition
10 9 8 7 6 5 4 3 2 1